W9-AXT-039

Jungle Doctor Paperbacks, No. F1

JUNGLE DOCTOR'S FABLES

JUNGLE DOCTOR'S FABLES

Paul White

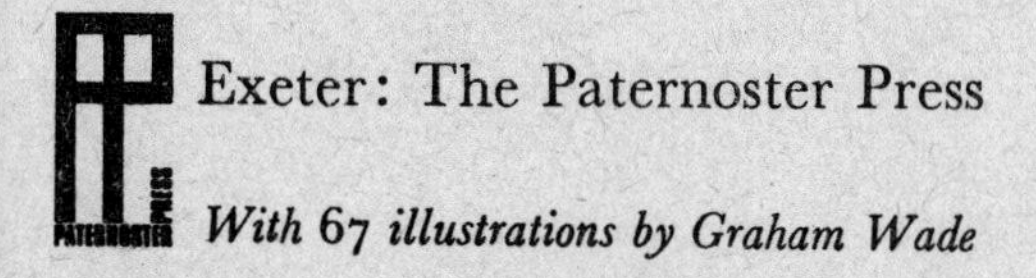

Exeter: The Paternoster Press

With 67 illustrations by Graham Wade

ISBN 0 85364 144 7

First published August 1955
Ninth impression May 1970
This paperback edition September 1972

Australia:
Emu Book Agencies Pty., Ltd.,
1 Lee Street, Sydney, N.S.W.

South Africa:
Oxford University Press,
P.O. Box 1141, Oxford House,
11 Buitencingle St., Cape Town

Made and printed in Great Britain for The Paternoster Press, Paternoster House, 3 Mount Radford Crescent, Exeter, Devon by A. Wheaton & Co., Exeter.

Contents

The deadly thing

DAUDI, a dispenser at Jungle Doctor's hospital, was making medicines for stomachs.

In the buyu tree outside the hospital, crows were quarrelling noisily. The shadows were getting long as the afternoon in Tanganyika wore on.

In the shade outside the dispensary door were those who recovered from various sicknesses. They were talking.

"I have strong fear of lion," said one whose leg and head were bandaged. He shivered slightly.

A long thin boy coughed and then said:

"*Heh*, the very thought of Nzoka the snake makes my skin go pimply."

A man who was recovering from malaria said in a tired voice:

"*Heh*, Kifaru the rhino with his feet that shake the ground, his fierce horn, his . . ."

Words failed as his teeth chattered in alarm.

Daudi weighed some white powder and poured it in a bottle.

"The creatures really to fear," he said, in a voice that carried, "are Mbu the mosquito and Papasi the tick and Hazi the fly. Small things, yes, but they kill a thousand times more people in a year than all the fierce ones of the jungle." Daudi stopped, absolutely still. "But there is another thing more deadly, more dangerous . . ." A visible shudder went through those that listened and

M'gogo, who came every day to the hospital for eye medicine, was very perplexed. "I shall tell you of this deadly thing in many ways," said Daudi, "for it is most important that you understand. How many sides has this tin?"

He held up a container marked "*Sodi Bic.*" Those who listened were cautious.

"Four sides," said one.

"Also a top and a bottom," suggested M'gogo.

Daudi nodded.

"Also there are many sides to this deadly thing. Listen."

d at Daudi the hospital
relight, his finger raised.
he night air.

in the jungle. All the
morning, under the shade
what could be done, for a
appeared right through the

ery broad and, as far as Twiga
n his vantage point, it was ex-

ungle is on that side," roared Simba
p shade of the green trees, the blue
ke, the cool of the small streams that
mountain. . . ."
into a grumble.
Twiga, "and on this side are thorns
rt, and even the water holes are muddy."
inoceros was furious. He snorted, his
es gleamed.

"*Koh*," he sniffed in an
wall indeed. I will charg

The animals nodded th
the way out.

'Faru walked back.

He turned and, runnin
work, galloped towards
short, pounding feet, hi
wall came closer and cl

His head was down.

Wham!

'Faru struggled back

The wall stood exactl

He was conscious of
dering.

Breathing noisily, he w
jungle. He braced his b
very big tree and started
before. The ground shoo
clouds, and he hit the wall

He staggered back, flat on
caressing his buckled horn.
above swelled visibly, his bead
directions at the same time, his m
the whirlwind.

"*Heh*," said Twiga the giraffe, by
"Truly this is a wall of great strengt

Nhembo the elephant waved his
tail in the same way, only less.

He trumpeted, "It takes strength
through a wall like that."

Up to the wall he walked, elephant fa
it with his trunk. Then his great sho
against it.

Chapter 1

The Great Wall

THE whites of many eyes stare
dispenser as he stood in the fi
African night noises came on t
Daudi's deep voice started . . .

THERE was consternation
animals met together one
of a great buyu tree, to see
great wall had suddenly
jungle.

It was very high and
the giraffe could see fro
tremely thick.

"The best of the ju
the lion. "The dee
water of the great la
come from the grea

His roar merged

"*Yoh*," lamente
and dust and dese

'Faru the rh
small beady ey

d out like a crosscut saw, "a
through it."
eir heads. This was, perhaps,

g as fast as his short legs would
the wall. Dust flew up from his
s horn stuck out fiercely. The
oser.

.

y as it was before.
many, many eyes watching, won-

alked back still further into the
ack feet against the trunk of a
to gallop faster than he had
k, the dust rose in greater
ker-whop!
his haunches, his front feet
The bruise on his forehead
eyes looked in different
ind spun like ifulafumbe

way of conversation.
."
runk to and fro, his

f shoulder to push

hion, and tested
ulder came up

Whock! Whock!!

Ker-bock!! Ker-bock!!

The wall did not budge so much as the thickness of his tail.

Nhembo slowly turned round and used the other shoulder.

Little puffs of elephant breath came spasmodically from his trunk as his shoulder bashed and bashed and bashed against the wall. Then he, too, sat exhausted beside 'Faru and placed pawpaw leaves over his blistering shoulders.

"Truly," came the words breathlessly down his trunk, "there is no way *through* this wall. It is a barrier of strength."

He walked away towards the swamp to find cool, soothing mud.

Mbisi the hyena laughed his ugly laugh.

"For animals of great strength and small nimbleness, this is a task too great for them. But as for me, I am a creature of subtlety. I shall find a way *around* it."

There was a sneer in his voice that caused many a hide to wrinkle in annoyance.

Twiga looked down from where he was nibbling shoots on the top of a thorn tree.

"*Hongo*," he said, his great tongue moving in and out a little more than it needed, "show us this way of wisdom."

Mbisi rudely turned his arched back and slunk off, following devious and winding paths beside the wall.

The sun set. Hunger came to the animals of the jungle as they waited, but Mbisi had not returned when the moon rose.

Another day came and they waited, and another night fell and still Mbisi the hyena did not return.

Again the next day, the animals of the jungle returned to the buyu tree and waited for the scavenger of the jungle to return.

'Faru had straightened his horn with difficulty and the help of Nyani the monkey. He was much encouraged by the work of Ndeje, the bird who picked the ticks from his hide and whispered words of encouragement into his ear.

Nhembo the elephant plastered his blistered shoulders with slime and gently poured liquid mud over his aching spine. He trumpeted softly and murmured consoling words through his trunk into his large left ear—words that sounded to others like distant thunder.

Twiga quietly ate the greenest shoots from the very top of the umbrella tree.

Nyani the monkey chattered and scratched with his relations and Nzoka lay curled up in the warm dust and thought of food.

At sunset, Mbisi returned, weary-footed, limping.

"*Yoh*," he muttered, putting

his head miserably between his front legs, "it is useless. There is no way *around* it. It goes *on*, and on, and on."

Nzoka the snake softly uncoiled himself, lifting his swaying head.

"*Kah*," he hissed, "you animals have strength and wisdom and speed to walk many miles but I, Nzoka, with my body that bends in all directions, will find a way *under* the wall."

A second later the animals watched his tail disappear down a hole that was close to the Great Wall that divided the jungle. They waited and watched, but all was silent in the jungle.

Time went by.

The crow sang his late afternoon song as he returned at sundown to the buyu tree.

The animals were about to return home for their evening food when a stirring of dust at the very foot of the wall caused them to stop and look. Many eyes were focused on the spot, eyes which stared and blinked and goggled.

Then Nzoka's head appeared. He faced the wall.

"*Heeh!*" he hissed, his tongue flickering with triumph. "I've done it. I alone of all the animals of the jungle have found my way to the other side of the Great Wall."

"Pardon," Twiga spoke gently, bending down his long neck, "but you are still on the same side as all the rest of us."

Nzoka's head hooded with anger. He swung round, red eyed, his words lubricated by venom.

"*Yoh*," his head darted this way and that, "I have travelled many dark ways under ground with skill and subtlety. No animal could have done as much. There is no way *under* that wall or I, Nzoka, would have found it."

"Truly," nodded Twiga, his tongue carefully within his mouth.

Nyani the monkey barked. "I will climb *over* it," he chattered, swinging his tail and loosening his muscles. With a whoop, he leapt at the wall, swarmed up, climbing higher and higher.

The higher he went the less there was for his paws to grasp. Suddenly his tail swung futilely, his paws clutched at nothing.

He started to slip. His body rolled over and over in the air.

Whock! He landed on his back at the very feet of Twiga the giraffe.

Nyani chattered for a moment as the breath came back slowly into his monkey lungs.

"*Yoh*," he said, scratching by sheer force of habit, "Twiga, stand close to the wall. I will run up your back and climb your neck. From the top of your head I will jump and thus climb with greater strength that I may go *over* the top."

Twiga was most obliging. Nyani

grasped his tail, swung on to his back, swarmed up his neck, leaped from his head and seemed to be going up and up and up but, again, far from the top, his clutch faltered and the animals watched as monkey's body somersaulted through the air to land flat—*ker-wham!*—at the feet of elephant. Nhembo did gentle artificial respiration with his trunk tip, then picked him up by the tail and lifted him up level with his eye.

"*Kumbe*, Nyani," he said, "is there a way over?"

"*Koh!*" said Nyani, speaking with the difficulty of those held upside down. "No one in the jungle climbs as I climb. Surely, no one can get *over* it."

So the animals tried but there was no way through, under, over or around that Great Wall.

Then it was they noticed the name of the wall, for it was written in faint letters which would be seen only by those who understood.

Twiga wondered strongly what it all meant.

"KAH," said Daudi, "but they were only the animals of the jungle. What is the name of the wall? There is no way to push *through* it. It is too high to climb *over*. There is no way *under* or *around* it."

One with a bandage covering his left eye answered, "The letters on the wall are S I N."

Daudi nodded. "Truly *sin* is the great barrier which separates us from God. But there are those who know that this Great Wall *has* got a way through it. There is a door. Jesus, God's only begotten Son, said, and said truly, 'I am the door. By Me, if any man enter in, he shall be saved.' Why should we stay any longer on the wrong side of the wall?"

Firelight shone on the faces of those who listened. Some nodded their heads slowly, but M'gogo supported his chin with his hands, for the words went round and round in his mind.

Chapter 2

Death trap

DAUDI cleared his throat.

"*Hongo*, only those who prize monkey wisdom get caught in death traps."

Those that listened nodded.

M'gogo listened with both ears.

Daudi went on.

PEREMBI the hunter set a trap. The trap was an oil tin with a hole cut in the top.

First the hunter put in sand and stones, then he covered this with a layer of peanuts. He placed it underneath a buyu tree in the jungle and went quietly away and sat in the shade and watched.

Soon many of the tribe of Nyani the monkey appeared.

The smell of peanuts was food for their noses. They chattered amongst themselves and then one, Toto by name, came close to look at the tin.

He shook it.

He peered through the hole, then put his nose to it and smelled.

Ahhh!! How good it was.

His monkey mind told him, "All you have to do is to put your paw through the hole and the peanuts are yours."

Toto looked this way and that.

He listened to the insistent voice of his nose.

His paw went rapidly through the small hole and grabbed all the peanuts he could hold.

Toto pulled his paw away quickly but it stopped with pain at the wrist.

The grasped peanuts in his paw would not come through.

Toto squealed loudly and the other members of his tribe chattered and squealed as well, giving much monkey advice in a variety of tones.

Toto strove with great vigour to pull his paw out, but it would not come.

Truly, the wisdom of Perembi the hunter was great in making the size of the hole.

Twiga peered over a thornbush. "Let go the peanuts, monkey," he advised kindly, "and your paw will come out."

But it was not the habit of the tribe of Nyani to let go peanuts.

Again Twiga spoke. "It is the peanuts that trap you. Let them go and you're free."

In the shade the hunter smiled to himself.

He picked up a bag made from baobab fibre, gripped his knobbed stick and walked slowly towards the monkey.

Toto in fear upset the tin and dragged it with him a little way but still his paw would not come out.

Nyani and his relations scurried to the top branches of the buyu tree, chattering.

"Let go the nuts and you're safe," again called Twiga, backing away.

But it is not the custom of monkeys to let go what they hold. (Such is the wisdom of monkeys.)

Toto squealed and drew back but the trap held him. Perembi the hunter swung his stick.

Kerwomp! Toto fell back, stunned.

His paw relaxed, the peanuts fell back into the tin and Toto himself was soon in the bag.

He had been trapped as he had followed his way of monkey wisdom.

* * * * *

THERE was a long pause. Daudi shook his head sadly and then spoke.

"Who can solve my riddle? What is the name of the trap?"

A whispering went on in the firelight. Then came a voice.

"The name of the trap is SIN."

Daudi nodded. "Truly. The words of the Bible are these: 'Sin pays its servants. The wages are DEATH,' and it is a matter of monkey wisdom to think that you can get away from this trap if you cling to things which will bring captivity and, after it, death."

The voice of Mbisi the hyena came eerily on the night air.

M'gogo shivered and thought many thoughts of small comfort.

Chapter 3

Safe as poison

DAUDI wrote on the ground

NUMBERS 3223

"Truly," said those that listened, "two and three are numbers."

"And so are three and two," replied Daudi.

They all laughed except M'gogo.

"Thirty-two is also a number as is twenty-three. The whole thing is a riddle," smiled Daudi.

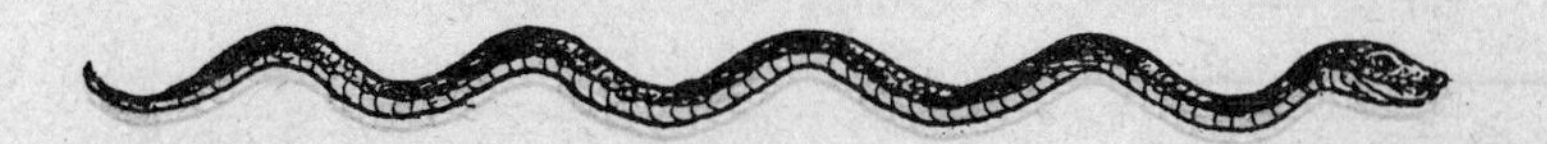

NZOKA the snake always had a famine within him. He complained to his wife.

"Behold, wife, there is never enough food to comfort my interior."

"*Yoh*," her tongue shot in and out like lightning. "Why, then, do you not get your own food?"

Nzoka hissed. "I have been thinking many thoughts. My stomach drives me to it. I *will* get my own food in my own way."

Said his wife, "Be careful. You will get into trouble. Your wisdom ceases where your stomach begins."

Nzoka hissed. "I will do what I know to be safe. *I* will not get into trouble."

"*Yoh*," his wife spat venom, "you certainly will."

"Female of many words!" scoffed Nzoka, wriggling his way through the warm dust and coming close to the house

of Perembi the hunter, whose son had seven chickens, the most industrious of which was Kuku the hen. It happened that Kuku had laid an egg. She was singing her song to prove it.

Nzoka, whose stomach walls stuck the one to the other, heard it. His beady eyes rolled and his tongue went out and came in with speed.

"The song of Kuku the hen means food, comfort for the sorrow of my stomach."

Silently he slid up to the house.

Now the mud and wattle walls of the house of Perembi

had suffered much because of the heat of the sun and the strength of the wind. The mud plaster on the wicker work had broken away at the bottom and there was one place where Nzoka could just squeeze his body between the sticks and the ground.

There, not far before him, beside the great grain bins, was an egg. He went up to it. It was deliciously warm, the sort of egg that brings joy to the interior of a snake.

Nzoka opened his mouth wide, his head moved forward, and the egg was swallowed. There it lay as a bulge, just south of his neck. Silently he moved to the hole in the wall. His head went through and also his neck but then he was stopped by the bulge that was the egg.

Gently he knocked the shell against the sides of the hole and instantly his interior was flooded with satisfaction.

Filled with content, he squeezed the rest of his body through the hole, the egg being deliciously distributed by the motion.

Home among the roots of the great buyu tree, he coiled up to sleep the sleep of the full.

He was awakened by his wife.

"*Yoh,*" she nagged. "What have you been doing?

Where have you been? What trouble have you got into?"

Nzoka twitched his tail angrily and his tongue flickered in and out with rage.

"I have my own ways and I follow the path of my own wisdom. My stomach sings a song of joy that it never sang when you cooked for it."

He closed his eyes but his wife went on.

"*Yoh,*" she said, "you be careful. You'll get into trouble. The path of your wisdom! *Kah!*"

She spat poisoned spittle.

Nzoka smiled a small smile. His stomach was at peace. His wife was full of words—*he* was full of egg.

Next day he again heard the song of Kuku the hen.

Again he found the hole in the wall of the house. Again he crawled through that hole.

Again he swallowed the egg and yet again his stomach was flooded with joy as he passed through the gap in the wall.

Later, seeing him lying curled and content, his wife came.

"Be careful, O snake," came her subdued hiss. "You'll get into trouble, make no mistake. Do things such as you are doing, and you'll get caught."

But Nzoka closed his eyes to the sound of her voice, his inner ears hearing but the contented murmur of his stomach.

On the third day, he listened for the song of the hen and swallowed the cause of her song. Again his stomach rejoiced within him. Again his wife warned with many words.

"*Kah,*" he said to himself, "there is no danger in this."

On the fourth day, seeing no danger, again he rejoiced, and his stomach within him.

On the fifth day, the son of Perembi the hunter said, "My father, daily I hear the singing of Kuku, but she sings without result. I will watch to see the reason for this."

The son of Perembi hid behind the grain bins. Kuku laid her egg and sang.

Nzoka the snake heard her song and followed his custom. He forced his way through the sticks. He looked to and fro hurriedly but there was no danger—there never had been.

He swallowed the egg, but the eyes of the son of Perembi watched him and in the mind of the hunter's offspring was born a plan.

Nzoka pushed hard against the sticks and the bulge just behind his neck burst, producing inward rapture.

As his body moved from the gloom of the hut into the bright sunlight of the outside world, Nzoka's wife said to her children,

"Here comes your gluttonous father, who follows the way of small wisdom, the way of danger, the way that will lead to trouble, to discovery, to . . ."

Nzoka hissed horribly and beat at his wife with his tail.

"Silence, wordy one!"

Perembi and his son thought deep thoughts and laughed with strength. The hunter took another egg next morning and placed it in water in a clay pot over the fire.

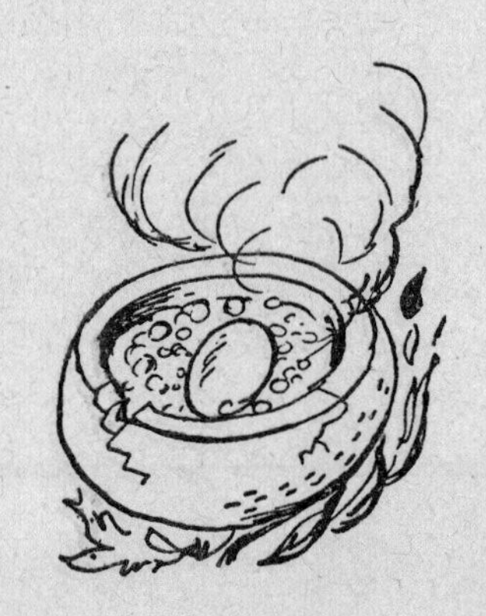

At the fourth hour, Kuku the hen came to her accustomed place.

The heat of the fire warmed the water and, as the warmth increased, the inside of the egg hardened.

Kuku sang as she moved from the place where it was her custom to lay.

Nzoka the snake heard the voice of her song.

The son of Perembi with speed removed the egg that had been laid and put in its place the one that had been in the pot. Each egg looked the same but within was a subtle difference.

Nzoka came to the hole in the wall of the house and pushed his way in.

On this day, he looked neither to the right nor to the left—his eyes were upon the egg.

"This talk of danger!" He smiled his small snaky smile.

Had he looked at the top of the grain bin, he would have seen the eyes of Perembi and those of his son.

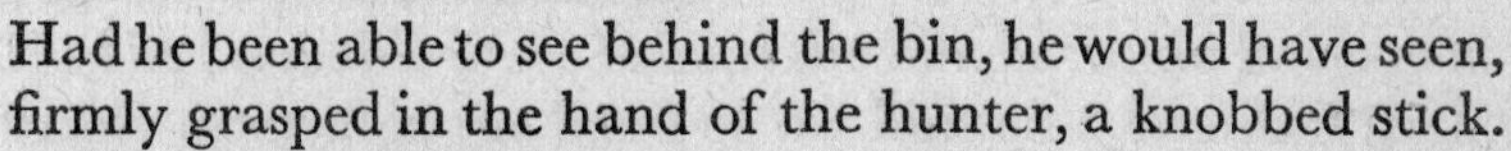

Had he been able to see behind the bin, he would have seen, firmly grasped in the hand of the hunter, a knobbed stick.

But Nzoka had eyes only for the egg, for which his stomach called insistently.

He swallowed it.

"*Yoh,*" he thought to himself, "Kuku the hen surely has fever today. This egg is hot."

He went to the hole in the wall and pushed his head out. He rapped the egg hard against the sticks.

"The shell of this egg has strength today."

He moved with greater strength against the sticks but still the shell did not break.

Again and again he forced his neck against those sticks. His strong body braced itself against the post that held up the roof.

In a frenzy, Nzoka lashed with his tail. But the egg was hardboiled and anchored him.

The son of Perembi laughed. "Medicine to cure thy stealing seems hard to swallow successfully, egg thief."

He came from behind the grain bin and—WALLOP!

At sunset the wife of Nzoka said to her children as they watched the body of father departing from the rubbish heap in the mouth of Mbisi the hyena:

"Behold, my children, do not follow the ways of your father. He said there was no danger. Because he had done it again and again and again, he said it was safe. But, behold, he travels now in the mouth of a hyena."

"*HONGO*," said Daudi, "you can't sin and get away with it. The words of the Book are these:

"'Be sure your sin will find you out.'"

"Which book?" asked one who listened.

"God's Book, the particular one called Numbers, chapter 32, verse 23."

In the deep shadow outside Daudi's house, M'gogo waited and spoke.

"My sin worries me. What must I do?"

"There is nothing *you* can do, M'gogo, but there *is* a way."

Chapter 4

You can't do it by yourself

"TELL me about the way out," said M'gogo. His eyes were very large. "I have fear of the deadly thing."

"You are wise to fear," nodded Daudi, "but with your ears wide open and the inner meaning of my words trapped within your mind, you'll find freedom from fear. You see, one day . . ."

NYANI the monkey and his relation Tuku had found a coco-nut.

They swung from tree to tree, throwing and catching it with skill. They scampered over the places where last year's corn stalks rotted. They chased it as it rolled down hill between the buyu trees and both stopped and chattered in agitation as it bounced off the high bank and landed plop! in the bog called Matope, the place of quick mud.

This was a sinister spot where even Nhembo the elephant feared to wallow for it was a place of deep sliminess that sucked down and down.

Tuku stood poised on the bank and saw the coco-nut well out of reach.

"*Yoh*, Nyani, I will get it back."

Bracing his legs against a stone, he sprang far out and landed close beside the nut, but in doing so, got mud on his paws. Following monkey manners, he wiped it off on his tail. Then, picking up the nut, he smiled.

"It is safe, O Nyani."

He turned to regain the bank but his left foot was stuck. Using monkey wisdom he pushed deeply with his right foot and before the word 'coco-nut' could be uttered, both his feet had sunk to the ankles in soft down-sucking mud.

Tuku threw the nut away. He struggled and screamed. Slowly the mud rose further and further up his monkey shins. In fear, he screamed to the monkey on the bank, "Help! Help!"

But Nyani, scratching fruitlessly in his agitation, could

think only monkey thoughts, so he merely chattered since it takes but small wisdom to chatter.

Tuku, sinking in the bog, cried, "Monkey, what shall I do?" But Nyani, now swinging by his tail from the lawyer vine, was deep in monkey concentration and slowly a monkey idea grew in his monkey brain.

Tuku struggled more and more and the mud reached up to just below his knees. The more he struggled, the more he sank; the more he sank, the more he struggled.

Then Nyani got his monkey idea.

"Tuku," he called, "you have strong whiskers. Grasp yourself by the whiskers and lift yourself out."

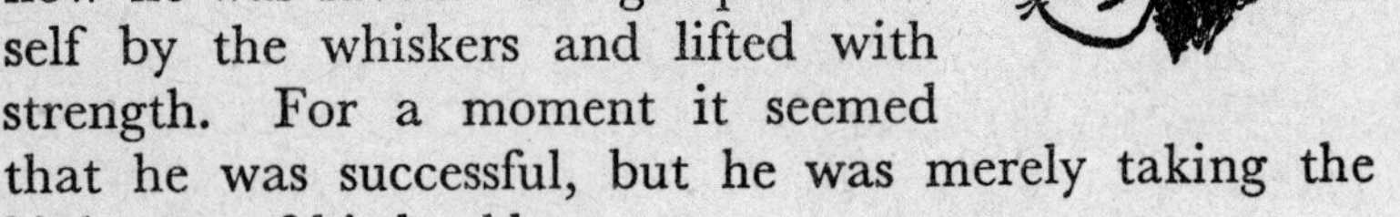

Tuku chattered with joy. Surely now he was saved. He grasped himself by the whiskers and lifted with strength. For a moment it seemed that he was successful, but he was merely taking the kinks out of his backbone.

The mud came up and up, past his knees.

The mud climbed slowly.

Tuku grasped at his whiskers and pulled again.

Nyani ran up and down the bank, screaming, "Lift yourself out! Lift yourself out!"

But the mud climbed and climbed hair by hair towards Tuku's hips.

* * * * *

Daudi turned to those who listened with wide-open eyes.

"Was it easy to get into the bog?"

They nodded.

"Could he get out by himself?"

"*Uh-huh!*" They shook their heads.

"Is there joy in being in a bog and in being sucked down?"

"*Uh-huh!*" Again their heads shook.

"And if he stays there long enough?"

"*Koh*, he will die. For a nose to go beneath the surface of Matope means death."

Daudi nodded.

While we were speaking, monkey in the bog is struggling and going down and down and the mud is coming up and up, and monkey on the bank futilely runs up and down, crying his monkey cry of "Lift yourself out!"

The mud comes up bit by bit.

It reaches the straining muscles of his arms, it presses on his ribs making breathing more and more difficult, it climbs up to the hollow under his neck. His throat struggles to swallow as the mud presses.

* * * * *

Dramatically Daudi paused, his hand raised.

"Was it easy to get into that bog?"

"Yes, yes, what happened?" The eyes of those that listened stood out.

"Could he get out of the bog by himself?" asked Daudi.

"No, no," they replied. "Tell us, what happened?"

"Was there joy to be in the bog?"

"How can there be joy in a bog like that?"

"What happens," asked Daudi, "if you stay in a bog like that?"

"TELL US!" shouted M'gogo.

Daudi went on.

The mud had reached Tuku's chin. He struggled frantically, fighting to keep his mouth above the slime.

But the mud came up and up. His small monkey nose was covered.

His eyes rolled frantically.

Clutching at his whiskers, he pulled and pulled again, but the last that his relation on the bank saw were two lone monkey paws clutching futile tufts of pathetic monkey whiskers.

And then the mud of Matope the bog smoothly and sluggishly came into place, and two small bubbles were all that bore witness of Tuku, the monkey who tried to lift himself out of the bog by his own whiskers.

A SIGH went up from those who listened, mingling with the night noises of the jungle.

Daudi turned round to them.

"What was the name of the bog?

"It's easy to get into.

"You can't get out of it by yourself.

"It makes you miserable all the time you're in it and in the end it kills."

The answer came at once from M'gogo.

"The name of the bog must be SIN, but how may anyone escape? This is my great fear."

Daudi nodded. "Once I was in that bog.

"I tried to lift myself out by my whiskers for I thought that what I *did* would get me out of the bog.

"The more I struggled the more I sank.

"And then I saw One beside the bank. I did not see His face but I saw His hand stretched out to me and in the hand, in the centre of it, was a scar.

"He said, 'Put your hand in mine, for I am the Way.'

"But I thought, 'Shall I do it? Shall I not struggle by myself and get out?' And then I felt the pull of the bog and I knew that those that stayed in the bog died in the bog, and I knew there was no way out but His strong hand, so I put my hand in His, and strongly He pulled me out.

"On the bank He said to me, 'Follow Me, for I have come to give you LIFE, better life,' and so I have followed in His way. Times have come when I have slipped back into the bog, but His hand was there to lift me out again.

"There is no profit in following any other than Jesus Christ. He is always there, His hand stretched out. He is very strong. All you must do is to put your hand in His and hold on. He does the rest."

Chapter 5

The monkey who didn't believe in crocodiles

"NO!" screeched Titu, the nephew of Nyani the monkey, "no! NO! NO! I don't believe it."

He swung from the limb of the buyu tree by his tail and made rude gestures at his uncle, Nyani, who scratched elaborately and successfully. He was suitably aloof from such insults.

Titu went on. "When I was young, O Nyani, you and others thought to frighten me by saying if I did this or did not do that, a ferocious crocodile with beady eyes would eat me. This dragon of your terrifying words was a creature huge as a fallen tree, with skin like drying mud, teeth sharper and longer than those of Simba the lion and a tail as strong as the nose of Nhembo the elephant."

"Titu, you are a small monkey of small wisdom," said Nyani coldly.

"Crocodiles are even as you describe them. They live in the still waters beside the river and they regard monkey, especially small monkey, as a choice morsel of diet."

"Yes, yes," chattered Titu, a sneer coming round his monkey lips, "tell me the rest. He has teeth that tear more than the claws of Chewi the leopard, skin thicker than Kifaru the rhinoceros, a mouth larger than Kiboko the hippo."

A gleam of anger came into Nyani's eyes. He leant forward and made a wild smack at the smaller monkey.

Titu swung out of range, laughing monkey laughter.

"Yes, yes, I know, but now I am grown. I know better than to fear the words of middle-aged monkeys."

In his rage Nyani ceased to scratch for a moment. Words failed him, so he swung high and far through the limbs of the kikuyu trees to the great grey rocks where he could sit and meditate on the rudeness of the rising generation and especially of small monkeys who didn't believe in crocodiles.

Seeing Twiga the giraffe eating green shoots from the top of an umbrella-shaped thorn tree, Titu climbed to the level of Twiga's head and greeted him respectfully.

"Twiga, have you heard of a creature of thick skin, of strong tail, of huge mouth, of beady eyes, that walks on land and swims in water?"

Twiga's long black tongue swept out, collecting some shoots, then he said,

"Truly you speak of crocodile, a creature of small charity and large appetite, that inhabits the pools and the swamps and the great river. I had an aunt once who . . ."

But Titu was chattering rudely, holding his hand in front of his nose in an unseemly way.

"*Yoh*, you have been talking to my uncle Nyani and he has told you to tell me this yarn. *Kah*, I do *not* believe in crocodiles."

He swung to the ground, ran nimbly to a flame tree where he noisily cracked the great pods and displayed his small knowledge of table manners. On a nearby bush was Ndudumizi the rainbird.

"Tell me, O bird of wide knowledge," Titu said, "have you heard of a creature large as a tree trunk, with a tail as strong as the nose of Nhembo the elephant, with claws sharper than those of Chewi the leopard, who has an appetite for small monkeys and lives by the waterside?"

Ndudumizi balanced his long black tail with care and said,

"O small monkey, the creature you speak of is undoubtedly crocodile," but before he could say another word, Titu threw the bean pod at him and scampered

away to a pile of rocks where Mbisi the hyena was accustomed to sleep in the daytime.

Now Mbisi had ugly habits and an ugly mind. In evil ways he was outshone only by the vulture in the whole width of the jungle.

"Mbisi," said Titu, "you are a traveller. You have seen many of the things that go on at night. Your nose is keen, your eyes are keener still. Have you heard of a creature large as a tree trunk, with skin thicker than that of rhino and looking like dried mud in the sun, a creature with beady eyes, a strong tail, a mouth of great size which particularly desires to eat small monkeys? I'm told and told and told that he lives besides the water."

Hyena laughed his ugly laugh.

"Titu," he said, "you are a monkey of wisdom. The old ones tell you stories to keep you from looking at your beauty in the calm of the water. What a creature you would look by moonlight in the still waters of the drinking hole beside the great river!"

Titu giggled to himself shrilly and moved as gracefully as he was able to impress hyena still further.

Seeing this, Mbisi said (and there was a sneer close behind his words),

"Prove they're wrong, O small monkey of great wisdom. Tonight the moon is at the full. Go to the place of smooth water and search for this fierce creature with huge mouth and fierce tail and skin beyond all comprehension."

With that, Mbisi crept slyly under the rock and went to sleep.

Titu could hardly wait for sunset, and then the moon rose. Slowly, with his monkey heart beating at a great rate, he went towards the placid water where the animals drank. He saw the pug mark of Simba the lion and almost lost himself in the footprint of rhino, and then he saw the water, silver and still.

He stood close to it and looked at his monkey face.

Entranced, he stared and, suddenly remembering his purpose, he said in a voice not quite as strong as he would have liked,

"There are no such creatures as crocodiles, nor ever were."

Behind him came a deep chuckle which made his hair stand on end, but he explained to himself that it was only Kwale the quail singing goodnight to those of his tribe.

Titu watched a log floating on the smooth water, a log that had dried mud upon it. It passed over to the bank beyond him and disappeared in the shadows and then he heard the rustle of the grass beside him.

"It must be the wind," he thought, although the water was unruffled.

Again he heard that deep chuckle.

"There are no crocodiles," screamed Titu, in sudden fear.

"True, O little monkey," said a deep voice, "how usefully true."

Terrified, Titu turned. There was a huge dark moving object, two bright gleaming eyes set wide apart. Suddenly a huge mouth appeared, gaped at him, showing teeth larger than those of Simba the lion. They moved

sickeningly closer. He felt a hot breath that smelled of swamps and stale meat.

"Ha!" roared a great voice. "I don't exist, eh?"

The great teeth moved forward a yard and the mouth closed. From between great teeth came the terrified chattering of a small monkey and a deep voice that said,

"I don't exist—no more shall you, little monkey."

THE night sounds went on uninterrupted for a full minute.

Daudi said, "Well?"

A voice came from the shadows. "Truly, crocodiles exist."

"And Titu?" went on Daudi.

"It was too late. He believed, but too late." M'gogo spoke huskily.

"Listen," said Daudi, "is it a word of wisdom to say, 'If we say there are no crocodiles, we deceive ourselves'?"

M'gogo nodded firmly.

Daudi's voice went on. "In the Book, it says 'if we say we have no sin, we deceive ourselves (behold, ourselves and nobody else) and the truth is not in us.' Beware that you do not follow the wisdom of Titu the small monkey."

M'gogo smiled quietly. He was beginning to grasp it all.

Title: Jungle Doctor's
Fables

Chapter 6

The small wisdom of feeding vultures

NYANI the monkey hated vultures.

But his second wife's first cousin Tichi was a creature of the smallest intelligence. He merely *said* he hated vultures, but he was fascinated by their sharp beaks, their featherless necks, the way their tails swayed and the curve of their dangerous claws.

One day a vulture alighted on the ground near Tichi's family tree.

His eyes drank in every movement of the foul bird.

He looked this way and that way.

No one was looking and he threw it food. Then, because of the voice within him which spoke loudly against vultures, he shouted in a harsh voice. With many gestures, he ordered it to be gone.

Next day, two vultures came. His eyes were hot as he looked at them, peering through a hole in the tree. His mouth was dry. Furtively he looked to see if he was observed but those of the jungle were not looking in his

direction. Again he threw food to the evil birds who came closer, squawking in a way that was not food for the ears.

Soon more vultures came and came closer, for Tichi repeatedly fed them. Then, in a voice that could be heard even in the far thornbush, he uttered threats to throw stones which would have been terrifying had he not thrown food instead. The vultures fluttered but stood their ground.

Twiga the giraffe from his vantage point above the thornbush saw all this and shook his head sadly, for he knew those who fed vultures sought trouble.

A week went by.

The vultures no longer stood at a distance. They came to the very foot of the tree, eating disgustingly the food which the small monkey furtively threw them. He watched them avidly, although fear stirred in his stomach.

In the noon heat of the next day, the bolder vultures were hovering above the buyu tree and though Tichi chattered at them in seeming rage, they squawked and fluttered awkwardly to rest in the tree, pecking savagely at the food he was about to offer.

High above them circled other vultures. All the time more and more of them arrived. They kept on landing and crowding closer and closer to him.

In real fear, Tichi beat about him with a knobbed stick, but to small purpose. The vultures he had encouraged were quickly overwhelming him. More and more vultures alighted.

They pressed upon him with their ugly heads and their tearing beaks, viciously pecking at his eyes, his body, his limbs. A

shrill monkey scream was drowned by the squawking of vultures.

At sunset Nyani returned from a journey. He was filled with horror to find the bones of his second wife's first cousin picked clean by the unclean beaks of the filthy birds.

"*Koh*," said one of those who listened, shivering. "Great One, I will sleep with dreams tonight."

"*Eh-heh*," said another, grasping the stool on which he sat. "I can see the head with its featherless neck pecking at me. *Yoh!*"

Daudi smiled and then became very serious.

"There are amongst you those that have told me that your trouble is thoughts which are not clean. The answer to my riddle is this. Feed these thoughts by what you look at, by what you read, by what you hear, by what you speak about, and they come hovering over and into your life.

"Starve them, and they go from you. Feed them, and they come in ever-increasing flocks.

"Many have the bones of their souls picked by these evil beaks."

"*Hongo*," said M'gogo to himself. "These words hit me with strength."

Chapter 7

Keep them flying

NYANI pressed his thumb against the limb of the buyu tree and again a *dudu* died.

The grandfather of many monkeys was filled with scorching anger. He chattered long and loudly as he climbed through the limbs of his favourite buyu tree.

He swung from a limb and confided his troubles to the ear of Twiga the giraffe.

"O Twiga, there are *dudus* of the baser sort in this buyu tree. Everyone has fleas; ticks are irritating, but at least respectable. But lice!—no!"

Nyani shuddered delicately, wrinkled his nose and scratched vigorously at the very thought.

Twiga listened with no little sympathy, moistening his lips with his long black tongue.

"No doubt the resting of vultures on the limbs of your family tree will account for this unhappy circumstance," he ventured.

Nyani flew into a rage and leapt from limb to limb.

"That bird of disgusting ways, that eater of carrion, that, that, that . . ."

Words failed him.

He trailed off into high-pitched chatter.

Twiga twisted his long tongue gently over the irritable tip of his black nose and remarked mildly,

"Should you act with firmness, Nyani, it is unlikely that vulture will alight on your buyu tree."

Nyani listened with interest and scratched with decorum.

Twiga went on.

"You cannot stop vultures flying over your buyu tree but you can stop them from roosting there."

Nyani thought for a time and the matter became clear to his monkey intelligence. Immediately he set about collecting stones to be kept in the hollow limb for use in such an emergency.

DAUDI threw some sticks on the camp fire. A shower of sparks lit up the faces of his listeners.

"*Koh*," said Daudi's listeners, "this, great one, is a riddle of depth."

The dispenser waved his finger at them.

"You can't stop them flying over. You can stop them roosting," he prompted.

A whispering went on, barely louder than the song of the cricket, and then one laughed.

"The answer, Great One, is this. For Shaitan the devil to whisper in your ear is not sin, but to stop and listen is a different matter."

Daudi nodded slowly. "Truly, temptation isn't sin. You can't stop Shaitan the devil's voice from reaching your ears, but to take notice of what he suggests and do it—that is sin. Look at God's words for yourself. The letter that James wrote, chapter 1, verse 12 and those that follow."

M'gogo murmured the reference over and over. At first light in the morning he would read it in his new book.

As the sun came over the baobabs, he read:

> "Each man is tempted when he is drawn away by his own lust and enticed. Then the lust, when it hath conceived, beareth sin, and the sin, when it is full grown, bringeth forth death."

Chapter 8

Out on a limb

M'GOGO had been looking through the dispensary window for a full hour. Daudi smiled as he made headache medicine. In a minute words would come.

"But how?" asked M'gogo suddenly.

Daudi looked up. "How what?"

"How can I get rid of my sin?" M'gogo's face was troubled.

Daudi labelled the bottle and then turned over the pages of a worn book.

"It says, 'Repent and be converted so that your sins may be blotted out'."

M'gogo rolled his eyes. "Words of difficulty, Great One, words that make my brain stumble."

"Tonight," said Daudi.

They settled round the fire after sunset, Daudi sitting on the stool M'gogo had brought. He started . . .

*   *   *   *   *

NYANI the monkey had a very fine jungle knife called *panga*. It was his special pride, and he sharpened it with strength and skill on the smooth flat stone underneath the meninga tree that grew beside the great granite boulders. The knife was so keen that he was able to shave the hairs off his tail with it.

Again and again he warned the small monkeys of his family tree.

"Do not touch *panga*. Should your paw so much as caress this great knife, then, small ones of my species, you shall taste of its flat in the place where your hair is least."

Now Tabu was a small monkey with twisted wisdom. He chattered and scratched and swung himself on to a high limb. As though *he* would touch the great sharp knife of Nyani, the eldest monkey of his tree!

The day came when Nyani was conferring with the other great ones of his tribe amongst the grey granite boulders and under the shade of the meninga tree. Tabu glanced at *panga* the knife and then he looked away.

Thoughts passed hurriedly between his ears.

Again he looked. His eyes told him how the edge shone, how strong and rustless was the blade and how smoothly polished the handle.

His eyes sparkled.

He touched *panga* with his forepaw. Truly, the handle was as smooth as it looked. His tail curled gently round that handle and *voh*! a thrill passed through his body. His tail tightened and quite by accident the knife came loose.

He leapt on to a higher limb, the knife held firmly. For a while he sat quietly on the limb, looking at the gleaming edge. His monkey mouth shaped itself into a smile as he saw how *he* could shave the hairs from *his* tail.

He nearly dropped the knife when unexpectedly the head of Twiga the giraffe appeared directly in front of him.

He greeted Twiga with the true courtesy of the jungle, and then, in a voice of pride, he said,

"O Twiga, I could cut through this limb with this great knife and the strength of my arm."

Moistening his paws with monkey spittle, he grasped *panga* firmly and coiled his tail tightly round the limb.

Wham! He struck.

Whim! Chips flew.

Twiga drew back hurriedly out of range, blinking his mild eyes.

"Be careful, O small monkey. Are you not on the wrong side of the cutting? Change your direction so that your back is to the trunk."

But Tabu was too busy to listen. He merely spat skilfully again on his monkey paws and chopped the more.

As the chips flew, Twiga's voice became more insistent. Slowly and distinctly, he said, "Little monkey, change your direction. With your back to the trunk you are safe, but where you are . . ."

With shining eyes, Tabu struck once more. A great chip flew past Twiga's ear. Little monkey grinned with triumph.

"With a knife like this——" he began, but then came a crack, sharp and terrifying. Tabu dropped the *panga* and shivering, retreated two monkeys' length down the limb.

"Hey!" called Twiga, his long black tongue twitching in agitation. "Tabu, come back. Cross the place where you were chopping. Change your direction. Go on to the other side of the cut, the safe side, the trunk side."

But Tabu shivered and chattered as the limb creaked again.

Twiga moved very close and spoke very confidentially.

"Tabu, it is a thing of wisdom to move back. Unless you change your mind about where you are, great trouble will come."

Again the limb creaked. Tabu moved further out.

"Change your mind, then change your direction," cried Twiga. "It's the only way."

But Tabu, dazed and frightened, shook his monkey head and ran out to the very end of the limb. It sagged.

"Quickly!" yelled Twiga, "change your mind, change your direction. Quickly!"

But there was a tremendous crack. The limb broke. Tabu fell, paws over tail, and landed, *whock!* on a great stone and lay terribly still on the ground beside *panga* the knife.

Twiga's eyes were full of sorrow.

"I told him to change his direction. I told him to change his mind," said the giraffe slowly.

DAUDI stopped. From his pocket he took a piece of paper which he carefully rolled up, lighted from the fire and put the flame to the wick of the hurricane lantern. He turned up the wick.

"You, too," he said, pointing from one to the other of those listening, "you, too, are out on a limb on the wrong side of the cut place. The Book says change your mind—that is, repent. The Book says, change your direction—that is, be converted. Come on to the other side, for the full words of the Book are these: 'Repent ye, therefore, and be converted that your sins may be blotted out.'"

Daudi got up and walked towards the hospital.

Those that listened sat quietly with their heads full of thoughts.

As M'gogo waited for sleep to come an hour later, he said to himself,

"I, too, am still out on that limb."

Chapter 9

Why God sent Jesus

DAUDI was making medicine for malaria in the dispensary when one of those that listened put his head through the window.

"Great One," he said, "why was it that God sent Jesus?"

Slowly Daudi put down the measuring glass.

"At the time when the birds of the jungle grow quiet, by the camp-fire I will answer that question."

* * * * *

THE birds in the jungle grew quiet. "*Hongo,*" said Daudi, "everyone in the jungle in this part knows my dog, Chibwa, a small animal with a cheerful face and an active tail."

There was a nodding in the half dusk.

In the days of the planting, Chibwa and I went to my garden to plant peanuts. At first we cultivated, I with my hoe, he with his back legs, and then came the days of planting. I had fashioned the soil into ridges and I came and planted. Then I found that, behold, Chibwa was following me, and as I planted he would come with his legs and dig up.

I turned to him and said, "Small dog." He turned to me and both his eyes and his tail spelt joy. "These peanuts that I am planting will be my food in the days of harvest. If you dig up the seeds, there will be no harvest.

Your master will starve and, because of that, you, too, will starve. It is a thing of small wisdom to dig up the peanuts that I plant, so please don't do it."

He wagged his tail and I said to myself, I have spoken with kindness and explained things. Now, behold, he understands and all will be well.

The next day, as I went to the planting, Chibwa came with me, and as I planted, with his feet he dug up peanut after peanut, so I went across to him and slapped him sharply.

In surprise he yelped.

His tail went sorrowfully between his legs.

There was no joy in his eyes.

"Dog," I said, with moderate fierceness in my tone, "dig up the seed peanuts and there will be no harvest and I shall starve and you, too, will have famine."

The small dog had shame and came and stood behind me, and I said to myself, "Behold, Chibwa now understands. The small amount of fierceness made the difference. I have explained it to him and now all is well."

The third day I put into my pocket a bone, a bone with meat on it, and I said, "It is a good thing to reward those that understand."

Again I planted and as I finished the first row I saw Chibwa move to the place and his feet were about to scratch but I came forward and gave him the bone with the meat on it. There was deep joy in his eyes and there was danger that his tail would wag beyond its limit, and I said to myself, "Now he understands. I have shown him kindness. He realizes that if he digs up the peanuts, then there will be no harvest. If there is no harvest I will have no food and he, too, will have no food and there will be cause of famine and grief and death."

On the final day of the planting, Chibwa came with

me. I had finished planting the first row when he started to dig up the peanuts. My mind was full of confusion and sadness and consternation, and I went and sat underneath the buyu tree and thought many thoughts.

And I said, "How shall I make Chibwa understand? I have spoken with kindness and with severity. I have given gifts. With every ability I have tried to make him understand. What can I do?" Then I said, "There is only one way. I must become a dog and talk to him in dog language. Thus I will explain it to him and thus he will understand."

As I thought these thoughts, I said to myself:

"That is why Almighty God sent Jesus. He became a man like I am, He was born as I was born, His boyhood was as my boyhood, His life was as my life. He lived that I might understand God. As I think of God, I understand Him when I think of Jesus Christ. He died when He was only thirty-three years old, a shameful death to overcome sin and to offer us the life that goes on for ever."

"Sin must be a very dreadful thing if God had to do that," M'gogo's voice came very quietly.

Daudi nodded. "Jesus underlined it with a great dark mark, His cross.

"Remember, He proved He was God by coming back to life again. *Kumbe*," said Daudi, turning to those who listened, "that is why God sent Jesus."

M'gogo was very quiet but his eyes sparkled as he nodded.

Chapter 10

Little leopards become big leopards

M'GOGO stood outside the dispensary.

"Great One, I have come for eye medicine."

"What of the eyes of your mind? Do you see the whole matter clearly, M'gogo?" Daudi asked, as he dropped black drops into two wide eyes.

M'gogo nodded, saying nothing.

"Then listen to the matter of little leopards and big leopards."

They sat on the shady side of the dispensary.

Daudi went on.

PEREMBI the hunter walked silently through the jungle. The wind blew in his face. In his right hand was a bow, on his back a quiver of arrows, at his side a hunting knife. Grasped in his left hand was his hunting spear, sharper than all sharpness. Silently he walked upwind, his eyes probing every shadow and bush. He moved through dense thornbush.

Suddenly he stopped.

There was a movement.

Quickly he fitted arrow to bow, but then he relaxed and spat with disgust. It was zebra that had made the movement, an animal of small profit to any hunter. Moreover, zebra's meat is an insult to the stomach.

His hunting was to find and kill Chewi the leopard, whose skin was worth many cows in the market place.

He moved on, the thornbush about him making the light appear mottled and streaked and striped. His eyes were keen as his spear, for Chewi the leopard could melt into such a background and not be seen until his strong teeth and his stronger claws had done great damage.

Suddenly Perembi moved into the shadow of a tree and froze into silent stillness. He had seen a movement.

Carefully he looked up, but his eyes told him it was only Twiga the giraffe, whose body toned with the light and shade, while his head stood out, nibbling daintily at the green shoots on the top of the umbrella tree.

Again Perembi spat and continued silently on his hunter's way.

And then he stopped. This time his spittle remained in its place. The arrow chosen from his quiver was the sharpest. Silently he moved behind the great trunk of a buyu tree.

His spear was ready to hand.

There, lying on a rock in the sun was Chewi the leopard. He fitted the arrow to his bow. His eyes sparkled when he saw that Chewi was of great size and of great strength. The spots on his skin were clear marked.

"Here," thought Perembi, "is great profit."

Carefully he aimed. *Twang!* The arrow sped. He leapt behind the buyu tree and came out on the other side, spear held in one hand, hunting knife in the other.

He was tense, expectant, but slowly he relaxed. A

smile came over his face for his arrow had sped truly and Chewi the leopard lay dead, his great muscles twitching.

Perembi walked forward and prepared to skin the great jungle cat. He tested the edge of his hunting knife on his thumb. It was very sharp. He planned where to cut so as to make least damage.

As he did so, an instinct within him produced its warning. He felt the hair on the back of his head stand up straight. He gripped his spear, turned and looked to one side and there, not two yards away from him, was another leopard.

Perembi was very calm. His knife flashed through the air, digging into the bark of imiya the thorn-bush. He stripped off a length of bark, knotted it and tied it gently round the body of the leopard, which was the smallest he had ever seen. He tied little leopard to a tree while he skinned the great leopard. The task completed, over his shoulder, held by the tail, was the skin of the big leopard, its great head dangling behind him. He took the bark with the little leopard attached to it and swung this also over his shoulder and walked home through the jungle with joy in his feet. He thought of the considerable profit that he would make from the sale of the great spotted skin. He thought of what he would buy. Now he was a rich one!

He said to himself, "Great fortune is mine, and truly I am a hunter of courage and skill."

He came to the village, singing his song of success. There were those that greeted him. The children shouted and laughed with amazement and joy. Then they saw the little leopard.

"*Yoh!*" they said. "*Heeh*, it is a sweet little thing. See how tender its eyes are."

Small hands caressed its soft skin.

"*Yoh*," they said, "it shall be our plaything."

The hunter laughed and went to show the great ones of the village the skin which he would sell for a large profit. Hearing of his success, the Chief came to greet. He praised the skill of the hunter. And then he came to the group of laughing children. Suddenly he stopped and lifted his spear.

"*Yoh*," he said, "a little leopard is not a creature of peace to have in the village. Behold, little leopards become big leopards, and big leopards kill."

But the children implored him. "Great One, do not kill our little leopard. See, it has tender eyes. See how it eats porridge from our hands. Its claws are too small to cause harm and see, its teeth, *yoh*, they are tiny."

The hunter, too, added his word. "Great One, it can do no harm. It is but a little leopard."

"Truly," said the great Chief, who was also the most skilful hunter in the whole tribe, "but it is true that little leopards become big leopards, and big leopards kill. Follow the way of wisdom and let me kill it now."

But they refused with strong words.

Day by day the children fed that little leopard on porridge and it grew. Its teeth grew, its claws grew, its spots grew, but it had the kindest eyes ever seen in the

jungle. The children played with it. It had no anger at the roughness of the very small children. Its tail would often be pulled, its ears, too, but still there was kindness in its eyes, and daily, at the hour of food, they fed it on porridge month by month. Its teeth grew and its claws grew and the spots became larger upon its back.

One morning to the house of Perembi the hunter came the Chief, in his hand his hunting knife. Out from the hunter's kaya came little leopard, now half grown. The Chief stepped back, his knife ready, but there were those that cried with loud voice,

"Great One, put your knife back in its sheath. Behold, this is our tame little leopard fed only on porridge, with the kindest eyes of any in the whole jungle. It is a creature of safety, it is the plaything of the children."

But the Chief shook his head. "Porridge or no porridge, plaything of the children it may be, but little leopards become big leopards, and big leopards kill."

"*Koh!*" said Perembi the hunter, smiling and rolling the leopard over with his foot and scratching it with his great toe. The animal purred deeply and wriggled in delight.

"Truly," said the hunter, "there is no fear in this little leopard. Others, perhaps, but not this little leopard. It's always been fed on porridge."

The Chief shrugged his shoulders. "You have heard my wisdom. It is the nature of leopards to kill."

But those of Perembi's family took no notice of his words and daily they fed the little leopard, and its teeth grew, its claws grew, its body grew and the spots multiplied in number upon its back. Its eyes were kind and did not lose their kindness, even when four children rode upon its back and steered it with its tail.

There were those in the village who shook their heads and said,

"*Yoh*, it has become a great beast," but Perembi the hunter only laughed.

"Truly, but it has been fed only on porridge. There is no fierceness in it."

In these days it ate porridge in great quantity and its teeth grew until they were longer than those which hung round the neck of Muganga the witch-doctor. Its claws were longer and sharper than the great 'wait-a-bit' thorns of the jungle. Its spots were black and clear cut against its golden coloured skin. Its long tail moved with grace and its eyes were the kindest eyes in the jungle. Then one morning the youngest child of the household wandered off down the path which led to the well. As he walked, the limb of a thornbush reached out and scratched his knee. A great red drop trickled down the leg and large tears welled from the eyes of the child.

Hearing his sadness, Chewi the leopard ran down the track. His long red tongue went out and licked the scratched leg. His eyes one second were brown and kindly and then, suddenly, steeliness came into them. His great paw swept through the air and the child, struck by it, rolled over and over in the thornbush, too terrified to scream.

Chewi the leopard turned and walked slowly back to the hunter's house, the great muscles rippling beneath his spotted skin, his long sharp claws twitching, his leopard lips drawn back from his long teeth. The first snarl creased the grown leopard's face, lighted by cold, cruel, cunning, steely eyes.

Within the house, Perembi was making new arrows, whittling skilfully with his hunting knife. In the shadow, he saw the coming of Chewi into the house. He raised his voice.

"*Nenda!*" he cried. "*Clear out!*" bending his head to smooth a rough spot.

In that second, Chewi struck with tooth and claw. Perembi screamed in sudden fear. Convulsively his hand grasped his hunting knife but such was the strength of the little leopard that had become big leopard that before three breaths could be drawn, the hand relaxed from its grip on the sharp knife. Perembi was on his journey to the ancestors.

Through the village rang the alarm signal. There were those that dashed and hid themselves behind mud walls. The once little leopard in his fierceness and strength and deadliness walked through the silent village.

From his house to meet him came the Chief, spear in hand. Quietly he said, "I had warned them."

And then the leopard sprang. The fight was fierce and deadly. The Chief was wounded in both his hands, both his feet and his side, but the leopard lay dead.

He called the villagers together and said,

"The leopard is dead. There is nothing to fear. Dead, too, is Perembi, for he neglected my warning that little leopards become big leopards, and big leopards kill."

Daudi turned to those who listened.

"What was the name of the great chief?" he asked. "This is a double riddle. What was the name of the leopard?"

M'gogo jumped up, in his eagerness upsetting his stool.

"The name of the leopard was sin because little sins become big sins and sins, big or small, kill. And the name of the great chief was Jesus Christ, the Son of God, for He was wounded in both Hands, both Feet and His Side. He died that we might be forgiven."

"Truly," said Daudi, "He was wounded instead of us and because He was wounded, we go free, or, as the Bible puts it, the punishment for our sins was on Him and by His scars we are healed."

M'gogo said very quietly, so quietly that only Daudi heard:

"By His scars *I* am healed."

The milk in the coconut

M'GOGO stood looking at the bottles in the dispensary. Daudi was counting pills. When he had finished, the African boy said:

"Great One, last night Nyani and his many relations visited me upon my bed. It was a thing of amazement. I could see the old monkey sitting on a great granite boulder while the five monkeys of small wisdom were before him. They seemed to be sitting on the limb of a tree that was not there." M'gogo paused, and then in an apologetic voice, "Great One, in my dream I could not see the limb but I could see the moon shining through the ghost bodies of the little monkeys."

Daudi smiled. "Truly it was a dream of interest."

M'gogo saw he understood and went on.

"Nyani was speaking to them. He said, 'In the village of the tailless ones is a maker of medicines who mixes stuff and pours it into bottles. The smooth-skinned ones of his tribe in their turn pour these medicines into their mouths and wrinkle their noses as does N'gubi the warthog.'

"'*Koh,*' said Toto, 'such is the wisdom of men.'

"'Quiet!' barked Nyani.

"The five unwise monkeys came closer together, shivering slightly. Nyani poised his front paw.

"'As I was saying, in the village of the tailless ones, Daudi tells words to those who listen. Amongst them was one M'gogo, of open ears and uncomfortable mind.

He heard tell of you, O Toto, and how you were trapped by monkey wisdom.'

"Toto looked uncomfortable and nibbled nervously at his back claws.

"'In his mind were fears of the trap. He slept broken sleep and he sweated cold sweat for he had no joy in traps or thoughts of traps."

Daudi smiled. "You realized you were a sinner, M'gogo."

M'gogo nodded several times and went on.

"Nyani looked further down the invisible limb.

"'Then he heard tell of you, O Tuku, and of your doings with a coco-nut and what happened in the bog Matope.'

"Tuku blushed a ghostly blush and caressed a depleted crop of whiskers. 'Truly, O Nyani,' he murmured. 'There was small safety in your monkey idea to save myself from the down-sucking mud.'

"Nyani suddenly became interested in the tip of his tail."

M'gogo leaned across to Daudi and whispered, "My fears became stronger when I understood that nothing I could do *would help me against the deadliness of sin."*

"'*Yoh*,' said Titu, the small black monkey, 'and did the tailless one hear of my unhappy belief that crocodiles did not exist?'

"The mere mention of the word made him look furtively over his shoulder. In the moonlight he half expected to see again a huge mouth and huge teeth.

"Nyani nodded solemnly. 'He heard, and his blood turned to water. For though he believed in both crocodiles and in what Daudi told him was worse than the huge reptile, he did not know how to escape.'"

M'gogo nodded. "My joy was small. My sin worried

me. I tried to forget it, to change the subject in my mind, but I shivered within and the thought of crocodiles made my skin clammy with cold sweat."

"'Tabu!' screeched Nyani, 'stop trying to spit on your paws. It is my belief,' Nyani was furious, 'that you would again stay on the wrong side of the limb and chop.'

"Then, as is the habit of dreams, it was no more."

Daudi smiled.

"It was then, O Daudi, that I commenced to understand that 'repent' meant to change my mind. I wanted to do so and to follow my mind with my whole living for, above all things, I wanted my sin to be blotted out."

Daudi nodded. "And what did you do?"

"I asked Him to blot mine out as a man rubs out footprints in the sand. He did, but as He did so, I saw the scars in His Feet and I thought of the cost and of the Cross.

"Then I thought of my dream and of your many words. Truly there is no profit in monkey wisdom, but *kah*!" the African boy grinned, "there is great happiness and joy now I am out of the trap, out of the bog, out of danger, through the door, and on the right side of the wall."

Daudi nodded. "Remember, your soul must grow now. Feed it daily." He tapped the Bible on the table before him. "If you would live with happiness, avoid little leopards and avoid feeding vultures. Live looking unto Jesus, the Author and Finisher of your faith."

M'gogo nodded. "Is not life like a coco-nut? It is but monkey wisdom for one who belongs to Him to continue chewing the shell when he has found that inside is meat and milk."

THE JUNGLE DOCTOR SERIES
Paul White

The Jungle Doctor books have become famous all over the world. Many changes have come to Africa since they first appeared, yet the instant appeal of a first-class tale, worth telling and reading for its own sake, makes them as fresh and lively now as they were when they were first published. A full list of titles appears below.

JUNGLE DOCTOR 0 85364 129 3
Christmas in Africa, with a thorn bush for a Christmas tree, and banana leaves as substitute for holly! Jungle Doctor, with a practice covering thousands of square miles, and an even larger number of patients, finds that the battle against tropical disease has its lighter side as well.

JUNGLE DOCTOR ON SAFARI 0 85364 053 x
"Sukuma" is Swahili for "push", and what better name could be found for the ancient car in which Jungle Doctor lurched from one crisis to another? Thrilling adventures could hardly be avoided in an unpredictable country where, in a few hours, a solid track might be changed into a sea of red mud, or a channel six feet deep might be cut across a road by flood water from the hills.

JUNGLE DOCTOR OPERATES 0 85364 132 3
"Do-it-yourself" could well have been the motto of the Jungle Hospital. A football bladder, some parts of a stethoscope, an ancient motor-car foot pump and an empty pickle-bottle provided, for virtually nothing, an anaesthetic machine!

JUNGLE DOCTOR ATTACKS WITCHCRAFT
0 85346 055 6
When little Mbuli was brought to the Jungle Hospital, everyone said it was a waste of time – the boy was bewitched, and would certainly die. But Jungle Doctor knew better, and soon Mbuli went home fit and well. Three days later he was found at death's door, abandoned by his friends. So the scene is set for an epic battle with the Witch-doctor.

JUNGLE DOCTOR'S ENEMIES 0 85364 135 8
A measles epidemic strikes, but Jungle Doctor finds himself fighting much more than a disease. Once again, Jungle Doctor and his African helpers find themselves up against it.

JUNGLE DOCTOR MEETS A LION 0 85364 136 6

Simba the lion-hunter nearly meets his match, but his life is saved in the Jungle Hospital. But Simba has to learn that there are enemies more dangerous than lions, and better ways of conquering them than the spear.

JUNGLE DOCTOR TO THE RESCUE 0 85364 137 4

When Simba the lion-hunter and his new wife Perisi go to live in an outlying village, their coming is deeply resented by some who had made a profit out of ignorance and disease.

JUNGLE DOCTOR'S CASEBOOK 0 85364 059 9

"I will give you a cow for this thing", said the deaf man who had faintly heard a human voice for the first time in years when Jungle Doctor yelled down his stethoscope into the deaf man's ear.

JUNGLE DOCTOR AND THE WHIRLWIND

0 85364 138 2

The lure of easy money overshadows the Jungle Hospital. The diamond mines and "the great peanut-growing" offer wealth beyond anyone's wildest dreams. But wealth brings problems with it, as Jungle Doctor and his African friends discover.

EYES ON JUNGLE DOCTOR 0 85364 139 0

Old Ng'wagu has his sight restored by Jungle Doctor and his "instruments of iron". But Berenge the witch-doctor, who has grown rich by his own brand of "strong medicine for eyes" sees his living disappearing as a result, and plots the old man's downfall.

JUNGLE DOCTOR LOOKS FOR TROUBLE

0 85364 062 9

Trouble seemed to be in the very air, but it was impossible to get to the bottom of it. In the village of a hostile chief an attempt was made on the life of Simba, and Jungle Doctor found him, with half an arrow in his back, only just in time to save his life. The trouble strikes the family of the chief himself, and Jungle Doctor is called in to seek it out and cure it.

JUNGLE DOCTOR GOES WEST 0 85364 140 4

Jungle Doctor is forced to take a rest, and goes off on Safari, accompanied by young Mgoba, who makes the breakfast toast in front of a fire, keeping the slices already made warm by holding them between his toes!

JUNGLE DOCTOR STINGS A SCORPION

0 85364 141 2

Nje – "The Scorpion" has a special hate in his life, the Jungle Hospital and all who work there. The only person to escape his hatred is Staff Nurse Wendwa, whom he wants as one of his wives.

JUNGLE DOCTOR HUNTS BIG GAME 0 85364 065 3

Bill Bailey, an American photographer who is immediately dubbed "Bwana Kodaki", Colonel Johnson, a well-known former big-game hunter and Jungle Doctor set out on safari to photograph big game on the great plains of Tanzania.

JUNGLE DOCTOR ON THE HOP 0 85364 142 0

A feast of eighty-seven roasted rats enjoyed by the boys of the tribe is the first hint that all is not well, and when news comes of a village where many are dying from a mysterious sickness that produces many "swollen places", Jungle Doctor recognizes the symptoms of bubonic plague.

JUNGLE DOCTOR'S CROOKED DEALINGS

0 85364 067 x

Enter Goha, the tragically deformed but irrepressible little boy, and Seko, his dog. Both of them seem to be surrounded by crooked things, and Jungle Doctor straightens them out.

JUNGLE DOCTOR SPOTS A LEOPARD 0 85364 143 9

This story begins with mysteries – mysterious deaths, mysterious diseases, mysterious threats, and especially the mysterious tracks of a four-toed leopard that is threatening the village. The tracks come nearer, until at last the leopard strikes, and Baruti the hunter realises that he alone can tackle it.

JUNGLE DOCTOR PULLS A LEG 0 85364 069 6

The winds of change seem to blow as strongly through the Jungle Doctor country as elsewhere in Africa. New arrivals include the "little box" that speaks to Nairobi in a second, and saves many days journey, not to mention the con-man, who tries to sell four artificial legs that once belonged to his "poor dead brother"!

JUNGLE DOCTOR SEES RED 0 85364 083 1

This is the story of the Wadoyek, a tribe which stubbornly tries to stand against the tide of history. Proud, self-sufficient, these nomadic cattle-rearers in their red garments, their hair daubed with red mud, stride through the pages of this story.

JUNGLE DOCTOR'S FABLES
Paul White

These classic stories have a magic all of their own. Above all, they are characterised by the hallmark of all great storytelling – they are a delight to six year olds as well as to those ten times that tender age!

JUNGLE DOCTOR'S FABLES 0 85364 144 4
There was once a monkey who didn't believe in crocodiles – but that did not make any difference when he met one in the middle of the night on the banks of the Great River. There was another monkey who tried to pull himself out of a bog by his whiskers – all that was left of him was two small bubbles on the top of the mud!

JUNGLE DOCTOR'S MONKEY TALES 0 85364 145 5
The wisdom of monkeys is proverbially small. They never *could* remember *not* to get too near to the hind feet of zebra, nor to throw coconuts at Chewi the leopard, nor to look into the eyes of snakes. Fortunately for his young nephews, Uncle Nyani, the sole survivor of a family of seven, is always there to do his best to knock some sense into their heads!

JUNGLE DOCTOR'S TUG-OF-WAR 0 85364 146 3
Even by monkey standards, Toto was pretty dim. The Jungle underworld, in the form of Crunch the Crocodile, Mbisi the Hyaena, Slinki the Jackal, Vibi the Vulture, and Gnark the Crow think he will turn out to be easy meat.

JUNGLE DOCTOR'S HIPPO HAPPENINGS
0 85364 147 1
Boohoo the Unhappy Hippo had a face which frightened even him when he looked in the mirror, and the rest of him wasn't much more beautiful! Unfortunately, there was a great deal of empty space between his strangely-shaped ears, and he suffered not only from a tendency to hay-fever, but from an equally frightful desire to Help People.
